WALKING RIBBON

By

Julia Taylor Ebel

Illustrations by

Cheryl Powell

To Annabel.
you have stories inside
you too! Keep them!
Julia Taylor Ebel
2005

VIEWPOINT PRESS, INC.
P.O. Box 430
Pleasant Garden, NC 27313

Special thanks to Francine Holt Swaim and Elizabeth Macdonald

Publisher's Cataloging-in-Publication
(Provided by Quality Books, Inc.)

    Ebel, Julia Taylor.
      Walking ribbon / Julia Taylor Ebel; editor, M.E. Smith-Ankrom;
       illustrator, Cheryl Powell.
      p. cm.
      SUMMARY: Nine-year-old Maggie takes her pet calf on a
    walk through Liberty, N.C., in 1898. The arrival of the
     daily steam engine train sends them home in a surprised
    hurry.
     Audience: Ages 6-10.
    LCCN 2004113385
    ISBN 0-9662431-2-9
     1. City and town life—Juvenile fiction. 2. Calves—
    Juvenile fiction. 3. Liberty (N.C.)—Juvenile fiction.
    [1. City and town life—Fiction. 2. Cows—Fiction.
    3. Animals—Infancy—Fiction. 4. Liberty (N.C.)—Fiction.]
    I. Powell, Cheryl. II. Title.

    PZ7.E1675Wal 2004   [E]
                QBI04-700501

Printed in China

To receive the Walking Ribbon Language Skills Booklet
send a self-addressed (9" x 11") stamped envelope to:

Viewpoint Press, Inc., Walking Ribbon Language Skill,
P. O. Box 430, Pleasant Garden, NC 27313.

In memory of Grandmother, who once flew behind a calf,
and for Uncle Joe, who long ago introduced me to the calves in his calf barn.
J.T.E.

Maggie skipped toward the house, clutching a handful of violets she'd picked for Mama. When she heard Papa's gentle voice inside the barn, Maggie stopped at the door.

"It won't be long till the calf is born," Papa said. He rubbed his hand over Bertha's bulging side.

Maggie Pickett lived in a white house with a big front porch near the middle of Liberty, North Carolina. Bertha, the cow, claimed the barn and field out back.

Every day the steam train that folks called the Shoo Fly came through town, right past Maggie's house, clickity-clacking and toot-tooting its whistle. The train carried passengers and brought mail to the Liberty Post Office where Papa worked.

When Bertha had not one calf but twins, Papa said Maggie could keep one and take care of it. The little calf she chose had a dark brown patch on her forehead like a velvet ribbon bow, so Maggie named her Ribbon.

Maggie took good care of Ribbon. At first she watched Ribbon drink Bertha's milk, but the little calf was soon big enough to eat the corn and oats Maggie gave her. Maggie checked often to be sure Ribbon had plenty of food and fresh water.

Maggie and her brothers and sisters went to school at Liberty Normal College, where children of all ages came to learn. When school closed for the summer, Maggie was glad to have more time to spend with Ribbon.

One afternoon in June, Maggie poured a bucket of water on Ribbon and began scrubbing her. Mama saw the dripping calf and threw up her hands. "I declare, Maggie May, that wet calf's likely to take sick!"

Maggie scrubbed a little faster. "I'll hurry, Mama. See?"

Mama shook her head and threw up her hands again.

Now that Ribbon was all shined up, Maggie wanted to show her off. Maggie tightened the rope she'd tied onto Ribbon's halter.

First, Maggie led Ribbon through the yard. They walked big circles around the house and little loops around the well and Mama's boxwood bushes. Ribbon followed nicely, so Maggie decided to walk around town.

Maggie stood tall as she led Ribbon down Railroad Street. She let her brown leather brogans give her long skirt hem a little extra kick as she strutted. Her brown hair bounced in time with her steps.

Along the way, she watched from the corner of her eye to see if anyone would notice her. When she saw her friend Rachel Coble, Maggie waved and Rachel waved back.

When Maggie and Ribbon passed Matthew Hardin with his sack of prized marbles, he called out, "Whose calf is that?"

Maggie was pleased to answer, "Mine!"

"I'll bet it's not," he said.

"I bet it is," she said and walked right on, not missing a step.

The day was bright and sunny, a perfect June day. Maggie's feet almost danced as she skipped along. Ribbon had to trot from time to time to keep up.

Maggie wanted Ribbon to see where Papa worked all day, so she led Ribbon to the railroad tracks. First, she looked to be sure no train was coming.

Then Maggie stepped onto the tracks, but Ribbon did not follow. Maggie tugged on the rope.

"Come on, Ribbon! You want to see where Papa works, don't you?"

Ribbon did not budge.

"Sweet Ribbon, it's safe now." Maggie made her voice silky and soothing. Ribbon's big brown eyes looked worried. Her hooves danced in place.

"Then we'll just go back home," Maggie said. She led Ribbon away from the tracks.

Suddenly, Maggie stopped and turned toward the tracks again. "Here we go!" she shouted.

With a friendly but persuasive slap on Ribbon's rump, Maggie took off running. Ribbon followed. They did not stop until they reached the other side of the tracks.

"That wasn't so bad, was it?" Maggie rubbed Ribbon's cheeks. Ribbon looked up and mooed. Maggie laughed.

Maggie headed toward the crossroads in the middle of town. She led Ribbon past the depot and across the street to the town well.

Maggie liked to work the pump handle up and down to make the water pour out of the spout. She let Ribbon drink from the trough while she pumped some water for herself.

As water splashed from the pump, Ribbon scooted over to catch some with her big pink tongue. Maggie giggled.

"This is mine!" she scolded playfully.

Maggie and Ribbon walked on down the main street to the little post office. As she stopped near the door, Maggie pointed inside.

"See, Ribbon," she said, "Papa comes here every day to be sure the mail gets delivered."

Papa looked out as Maggie and her calf stepped right up to the door.

"Now, Maggie, don't you bring that calf in here!" he warned her, shaking his finger in pretended sternness.

Maggie just giggled. "Ribbon wants to see where you work." She patted Ribbon's head. Ribbon mooed and a man inside looked up in surprise.

On they went, little Maggie Pickett in her long dress and brogans, with brown curls bouncing, towing a calf on the end of a rope. They passed the bank, the millinery, and the shoemaker's shop. They walked across from the Liberty Mercantile Company where Mr. Griffin sold linen cloth and nails and flour and almost anything a person might need. Ribbon walked a bit faster every time a horse-drawn wagon clanked along the dirt street.

At the end of the block, Maggie and Ribbon turned and crossed the street. Grandpa Wrightsell's grocery store stood near the corner. Sometimes Grandpa gave Maggie a treat, and she secretly hoped he would offer one this day.

Maggie peeked in the front door. Grandpa greeted her from the back corner where he was stacking bags of cornmeal fresh from the mill.

"Well, Missy, what can I do for you today?"

"We're just out for a stroll, Grandpa," Maggie answered.

"Nice day for a stroll, but I reckon you could use a little nourishment for your efforts."

Grandpa disappeared for a moment and then returned with a shiny red apple and a little sack of grain. "For you and your friend." He nodded toward Ribbon.

"Thank you!" Maggie replied, and off she skipped with Ribbon trotting behind her.

At the corner she stopped for a bite of apple. "Would you like a nibble?" she said, holding out a handful of grain for the calf.

Maggie could see Dr. Patterson's house and office down the street. She remembered when Dr. Patterson had given her that awful medicine for the croup back in the winter. Thinking about the croup made Maggie remember what Mama had said about Ribbon's bath.

"You wouldn't get sick, would you, Ribbon?" Maggie asked.

The farther Maggie walked, the more she worried. She decided to take Ribbon to see Dr. Patterson just in case.

As she neared Dr. Patterson's office, Maggie could see the doctor at his desk by the window.

"Dr. Patterson! Dr. Patterson!" Maggie called.

Dr. Patterson waved and came to meet her at the door.

"What's the matter, Maggie?"

"I gave Ribbon a bath, and Mama said I'd make her sick. Oh, Dr. Patterson, that just can't happen!"

Dr. Patterson looked at Ribbon. He slid his hand across her head and down her back. He leaned down, placing his ear against her side to listen. He looked inside her mouth as Ribbon wiggled her thick, rough tongue.

"She looks fine," he said with a wink. "Just keep her warm and dry."

Maggie sighed with relief. "Thank you!" she said.

As Maggie skipped away, Ribbon mooed a calf-sized moo and trotted along to keep up. Maggie led Ribbon back toward the railroad tracks. As they neared the track, Maggie walked faster, but Ribbon walked more slowly.

"Oh, no you don't!" Maggie slapped Ribbon on the rump and took off running straight for the tracks. So did Ribbon.

"Now, that was quite a fine jump, Ribbon," Maggie said as all six feet, Maggie's and Ribbon's, were firmly planted on the homeward side of the railroad tracks.

They turned toward Maggie's house.

On the way they came upon Miss Liddy Brower working in her garden. Maggie waved proudly.

"Good gracious!" Miss Liddy said, standing straight up.

The only polite thing to do, of course, was to make proper introductions. "Miss Liddy, I'd like to introduce my calf. Ribbon, this is Miss Liddy," Maggie said.

"Pleased to meet you, Ribbon," Miss Liddy said and nodded to the calf.

Ribbon stretched toward one of Miss Liddy's pink dahlias as if trying to smell the flower.

"Isn't this a pleasant stroll?" Maggie exclaimed as they walked on down Railroad Street. Maggie started to hum a little tune.

That's when the Shoo Fly rolled into town, toot-tooting its whistle, puffing sooty black smoke, and clickety-clacking down the track. Oh, it made an awful racket!

Suddenly, Ribbon lit out running, just high-tailing it toward home!

"Stop, Ribbon! Stop!" Maggie shouted, but Ribbon did not stop. She ran as the train was coming, and she ran as the train passed beside them. All the way up the street, Ribbon ran. Hard as little Maggie tried, she couldn't keep her feet on the ground, and she couldn't run fast enough to keep up. She never did let go of that rope, though—not for one second! What a sight they were—Ribbon running in front and Maggie flying along behind, her toes barely touching the ground every now and again!

Ribbon turned toward Maggie's house but ran on past it, past the well, past Mama's boxwood bushes, and right into the barn—and there she stopped. Maggie's heart pounded as she flopped on the hay beside Ribbon. Ribbon mooed.

Suddenly Mama appeared at the barn door, followed by Maggie's wide-eyed brothers and sisters. Mama's hands covered her mouth as she tried to keep from laughing.

"Are you all right, Maggie?" Mama asked.

Maggie took a deep breath and sighed. Then she nodded and both she and her mother burst into laughter. Maggie's brothers and sisters joined in.

Maggie reached over and placed her hand on Ribbon. She looked straight into Ribbon's big brown eyes.

"Ribbon," Maggie said. "I thank you for escorting me to town. It was a most exciting stroll, but I think I may just be too busy to go again tomorrow. I hope you'll understand."

Ribbon nudged Maggie's chin gently and licked it with her rough tongue. Maggie just giggled.

Author's Note

Maggie May Pickett was a real girl, born in 1889 in Liberty, North Carolina. She grew up to become Margaret Pickett Hamlin, a teacher and mother of my mother. I remember hearing her laugh as she told me how her mother, my great-grandmother, had seen her flying along behind her pet calf. Maggie's mother told her what a hilarious sight the two had been, and Maggie, my grandmother, in turn, passed along the embellished story.

I, too, am taking my turn to fill in some gaps in the story and pass it along. Stories must be told if heritage and history are to remain with us.

Liberty has grown since the end of the 1800's. The post office has had several homes. The train station has been moved. The Liberty Normal College no longer teaches young children to read and write or prepares older students for business, teaching, or university study. A modern bank stands at the site of the old town well. Still the flavor of the earlier small town remains and is reflected in a number of older homes, churches, and other buildings. Among these is the home of Maggie Pickett's family.